To the Kids at
Parachute Library

Happy Reading —

Amy Krouse

For Mom
Para Mi Madre

Copyright 2003 Amy Krakow
ISBN #0-9715224-1-3
LCCN #-2003108741
Illustration Copyright by Steve Williams
graphictraffic@yahoo.com
Illustrations were done in watercolor, pen and ink and colored pencil.
Cover design and layout by James Kosmicki
Font is Garamond
Printed in the United States of America by
Walsworth Publishing Company

Wagging Tales Publishing
Box 691
Carbondale, Colorado 81623
amykrakow@hotmail.com

THE Mutt AND THE Monster GO TO MEXICO

LA Mutt Y LA Monster VAN A MÉXICO

Written by Amy Krakow
Illustrations by Steve Williams
Translations by Jill Knaus

When Lucy told me we were going on vacation to Mexico my tail wouldn't stop wagging. Finally I would have Lucy all to myself like the good old days before the Mutt showed up but then I found out she was coming too.

Cuando Lucy me dijo que íbamos de vacaciones a México, yo no podía parar de menear la cola. Finalmente Lucy y yo estaríamos solos, como en los tiempos pasados y antes de que la Mutt llegó pero luego yo supe que ella iba a venir también.

When it was time to pack, the Mutt brought her water wings, her Walkman and Soudee her Teddy bear.

Cuando fue la hora de hacer la maleta, la Mutt trajo sus aletas para el aqua, su Walkman y Soudee, su osito de peluche.

When we had our passport pictures taken the Mutt took so long grooming herself that the photographer fell asleep. By the time it was my turn I couldn't wake him up so Lucy had to glue an old picture of me on my passport.

Cuando sacaron las fotos de pasaporte, la Mutt perdió mucho tiempo arreglándose y el fotográfo se durmió. Cuando me tocó a mí, yo no podía despertarle pues Lucy tuvo que pegar una de mis fotos viejas en el pasaporte.

On the plane Lucy let the Mutt sit next to the window and she never even let me look out.

En el avión, Lucy permitió que la Mutt se sentara al lado de la ventanilla y ella no me permitió mirar afuera.

When we arrived in Mexico Lucy let the Mutt stamp her paw in her passport first. The Mutt took so long that when it was my turn they ran out of ink.

Cuando llegamos a México, Lucy permitió que la Mutt estampara la pata en su pasaporte primero. Duró tanto tiempo que cuando me tocó, no había tinta.

When we arrived at our palapa, Lucy let the Mutt play on the beach while I had to help her unpack everything.

Cuando llegamos a nuestra palapa, Lucy permitió que la Mutt jugara en la playa mientras yo tenía que ayudarla a sacar todas las cosas de las maletas.

When Lucy took us to visit the ancient ruins the Mutt thought she saw a ghost so Lucy held her paw the whole time and just ignored me.

Cuando Lucy nos llevó a visitar las ruinas antiguas, la Mutt pensó que vio un fantasma por eso Lucy tomó su pata y me ignoró.

When we went to the beach Lucy made me put on gobs of sunscreen and sit under a gigantic palm tree for an hour and a half before she let me play in the water. The Mutt never had to put on sunscreen.

Cuando fuimos a la playa, Lucy me puso mucho bronceador y yo tenía que sentarme abajo de una palmera gigante por una hora y media antes de que ella me dejara jugar en el agua. La Mutt nunca tenía que ponerse el bronceador.

Finally Lucy let me go snorkeling. It was really cool. I saw ten sharks and a school of jellyfish but then I got really scared because I saw the *ugliest* fish I had ever seen. It looked just like the Mutt.

Finalmente Lucy me permitió ir a bucear. Fue muy suave. Vi diez tiburones y un grupo de medusas pero luego me dio miedo porque vi al pez *más feo* que yo nunca jamás había visto. Se parecía a la Mutt.

When Lucy took us out to dinner she let the Mutt order our dinner in Spanish. I didn't know she could speak Spanish! The waiter brought the Mutt six beef burritos, five chicken enchiladas and about a hundred fish tacos. All I got was a dried up tortilla and a bowl of water.

Cuando Lucy nos llevó a cenar, la Mutt pidió nuestra comida en español. ¡Yo no sabía que ella podía hablar español! El mesero le trajo a la Mutt seis burritos de carne, cinco enchiladas de pollo y más y menos cien tacos de pescado. Pues él me sirvió una tortilla seca y un plato de aqua.

Before we went home Lucy gave me some pesos to buy a souvenir but I was so hungry I spent all of my money on food while the Mutt bought some silly postcards and a sombrero that would fit a Chihuahua.

Antes de ir a casa, Lucy me dio unos pesos para comprar un recuerdo pero yo tenía tanta hambre que yo gasté todo el dinero en comida mientras la Mutt compró unas tarjetas postales muy tontas y un sombrero que le quedaría un Chihuahua.

On the plane ride home I dreamt that Lucy left the Mutt in one of the Mexican schools so she could learn more Spanish but when I woke up the Mutt was still on the plane cuddling next to Lucy.
Sometimes it feels like Lucy loves the Mutt more than me…… even in Mexico.

Cuando regresamos en el avión a casa, yo soñé que Lucy dejó a la Mutt en una de las escuelas mexicanas para que pudieria aprender más español pero cuando me desperté la Mutt todavía estaba en el avión, abrazando a Lucy. A veces parece que Lucy quiere a la Mutt más que yo . . . aun en México.

15

Yeah…. yeah…. yeah. That's what the Monster says but here's the "real" story. When Lucy told me I could go to Mexico with her I couldn't believe my ears. I was the happiest dog in the world until she told me the Monster was coming too.

Sí . . .sí . . .sí. Eso es lo que dice la Monster pero aquí está el cuento "verdadero". Cuando Lucy me dijo que yo podía ir a México con ella, yo no podía creerlo.

When it was time to pack, the Monster filled her entire doggie pack with dog food and treats. I told her there was food in Mexico but she didn't believe me.

Cuando fue la hora de hacer la maleta, la Monster llenó su mochila con comida de perro y meriendas. Le dije que había comida en México pero ella no me creyó.

When we had our passport pictures taken Lucy brushed my fur a million times and the flashbulb was so bright it really hurt my eyes and then I forgot to smile. The Monster got to choose one of her own pictures from home and she looked really good while I looked like a poodle.

Cuando sacaron las fotos del pasaporte, Lucy cepilló mi pelo millones de veces y el flash fue tan brillante que me dolieron los ojos y se me olvidó sonreír. La Monster escogió una de sus propias fotos y ella parecía muy guapa mientras yo parecía un perro de lanas.

When we got on the plane Lucy made me sit next to the window even though she knows I'm afraid of heights and the Monster got to sit on the end where she could see everything and talk to everyone.

Cuando subimos al avión, Lucy me hizo sentarme al lado de la ventanilla aunque ella sabe que yo tengo miedo a la altura y la Monster se sentó al final de la línea donde ella podía ver todo y hablar con toda la gente.

When we had our passports stamped it really hurt and I got permanent ink all over my paws and the Monster never even had to get hers stamped.

Cuando estamparon nuestros pasaportes me dolió mucho y había tinta permanente en mis patas y no estamparon ni una pata de la Monster.

When we arrived at our palapa, Lucy let the Monster help her do everything and told me to take a walk on the beach all by myself. I cut my paw on a seashell and she didn't even give me a band-aid.

Cuando llegamos a nuestra palapa, Lucy dejó a la Monster ayudarle hacer todo y ella me dijo que yo caminara solita en la playa. Me corté una pata con una concha y ella no me dio una curita.

When Lucy took us to see the ancient ruins she let the Monster dig up an *old, old, old* bone but she wouldn't even let me go exploring.

Cuando Lucy nos llevó a ver unas ruinas antiguas, ella le permitó que la Monster desenterrara un hueso muy, muy *viejo* pero ella no me permitió explorar.

When we went to the beach the Monster and Lucy sat under a beautiful palm tree sipping fruit drinks with cute little umbrellas floating on top. I wasn't having much fun and I was too scared to go in the water.

Cuando fuimos a la playa la Monster y Lucy se sentaron abajo de una palmera hermosa tomando una bebidas de fruta con unos paraguas suaves flotando en las bebidas. No me divertí y tenía miedo de entrar en el agua.

I finally decided to put on my water wings and go snorkeling. It was really cool. I saw three stingrays and a Portuguese-man-of war but then I got really scared because I saw the *ugliest* fish I had ever seen. It looked just like the Monster.

Finalmente decidí ponerme las aletas para ir a bucear. Fue muy suave. Vi tres medusas y un pez horrible que me dio mucho miedo porque era el pez *más feo* que yo nunca jamás había visto. Se parecía a la Monster.

When Lucy took us out to dinner she made me order our meal in Spanish. I was so nervous that I ordered myself a giant beef burrito, a chicken enchilada and two fish tacos…… and I'm a vegetarian! I wanted to trade with the Monster but Lucy wouldn't let me.

Cuando Lucy nos llevó a cenar, ella me hizo pedir nuestra cena en español. Yo estaba tan nerviosa que pedí un burrito grande de carne, una enchilada de pollo y dos tacos de pescado . . . y soy vegetariana. Yo quería cambiar la comida con la Monster pero Lucy no me permitió.

Before we went home Lucy gave me some pesos to buy a souvenir. I bought a beautiful sombrero and some postcards but the Monster used her pesos to stuff her mouth with giant sized tacos.

Antes de regresar a casa. Lucy me dio unos pesos para comprar un recuerdo. Compré un sombrero hermoso y unas tarjetas postales pero la Monster gastó su dinero en unos tacos gigantes.

On the plane ride home I dreamt that Lucy left the Monster in Mexico and I sent her one of my postcards. But when I woke up she was still on the plane cuddling next to Lucy.
Sometimes it feels like Lucy loves the Monster more than me…... even in Mexico.

Cuando regresamos en el avión a casa, soñé que Lucy dejó a la Monster en México y le mandé unas de mis tarjetas postales. Pero cuando me desperté, ella todavía estaba en el avión abrazando a Lucy.
A veces parece que Lucy quiere a la Monster más que yo . . . aun en México.

Kids Comment on THE Mutt AND THE Monster

"Quiero este libro porque es muy chistoso y divertido para los niños."

Diego Beltran

"I like the part where the Monster digs out the old, old, old bone because she might get rich or super rich."

Jaime Chavez

"I thought the story was hilarious but I think you should write a final book where the Mutt and the Monster finally make up."

Matthew Piccolo

"I really liked the book because it was funny and exciting."

Jessica Miller

"I love this story. It is funny when the Mutt and the Monster bump into each other and think they're the ugliest fish. I hope you write another book."

Keith McCutcham

"I think your book is great. I love the part when the Mutt put on that small hat….it was so funny."

Dani Pyle

CANINE COMMENTS

"The Mexico vacation sounded great especially the part where the Monster got to dig up a really old bone. I wonder if she got into trouble?"

Lucky-Lab-mix

"The Mutt is so lucky to be bi-lingual. Maybe she'll teach me Spanish…all I can say is perro de caliente."

Percy- Terrier

"I helped Lucy choose that crummy old photo she glued onto the Monster's passport. I felt really sorry for the Monster because the Mutt's picture was so much cuter."

Emma- Lab

"I can't believe the Monster thought the Mutt was an ugly fish. The Mutt is so adorable especially when she's holding her little Teddy Bear."

Zoey-mix

"My sister Tres is just like the Mutt. Not only does she hog all the hugs but she's afraid of the water and it really embarrasses me when she wears her water wings."

Junior-Beagle

"My owner Jaime and I were in Mexico the same time as the Mutt and the Monster. Those two are not fooling anyone. I saw them snorkeling together and it looked like they were having lots of fun."

Peyton-mix

Mutt (a.k.a. Sparky) • Monster (a.k.a. Spooner)

The Mutt and Monster, more commonly known as Sparky and Spooner live in Carbondale, Colorado. These adorably sweet canines were the inspiration for this book. Based on a true story the Mutt and the Monster really do like one another, they just don't want anyone to know it.

Partial proceeds from this book go to Valley Dog Rescue, an organization in the Roaring Fork Valley that shelters and protects unwanted dogs until they can be adopted. Special thanks to those heroes who have worked endlessly to save the lives of so many animals. To visit their web site go to (*http://welcome.to/vdr*). Having a no kill policy and being a non-profit means that some dogs have to wait for a very long time before they can finally "go home."

For donations please send check or money order to:

Dog Rescue Fund
Bank of Colorado
Box 520
Glenwood Springs, CO 81602
Acct.# 5930047589

ORDER FORM

THE MUTT AND THE MONSTER GO TO MEXICO is a 32 page bilingual children's picture book written by Amy Krakow and Illustrated by Steve Williams.

It is the story of two dogs competing for the attention of their young owner Lucy, while on vacation in Mexico. Both the Mutt and the Monster think that Lucy loves the other one more than herself in this comical tale of canine sibling rivalry.

Quantity   Price

_____   The Mutt And The Monster Go To Mexico $ 15.00 per book

_____   The Mutt And The Monster $ 15.00 per book

                 Shipping & Handling $1.75 per book

                 Total Amount Enclosed $_____

Name and Address   _____

                   _____

                   _____

                   _____

Check payable to Wagging Tales Publishing • Box 691, Carbondale, CO 81623
Please include this order form with check or money order.
This page may be copied